MATT A

YUCK

YUCK'S SUPERCOOL SNOTMAN

AND

YUCK'S DREAM MACHINE

Illustrated by Nigel Baines

www.yuckweb.com

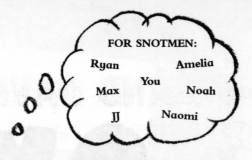

FOR SNOTMEN:

Ryan   Amelia

You

Max   Noah

JJ   Naomi

SIMON AND SCHUSTER

First published in Great Britain in 2008
by Simon & Schuster UK Ltd
A CBS COMPANY
1st Floor, 222 Gray's Inn Road, London WC1X 8HB

1 3 5 7 9 10 8 6 4 2

A CIP catalogue record for this book is
available from the British Library

ISBN 978-1-8473-8288-7

Printed and bound in Great Britain by
Cox & Wyman Ltd Reading Berkshire

www.simonsays.co.uk
www.yuckweb.com

There was a boy so disgusting they called him Yuck

YUCK'S SUPERCOOL SNOTMAN

Yuck blew two runny snot bubbles from his nostrils. He licked them with the tip of his tongue. The snot tasted juicy and sweet.

He sneezed. "**ATCHOO!**"

Sticky green snot splattered his duvet.

Just then, Mum came into his room. "Yuck, that's disgusting!" she said. "Have you got a cold?"

"I'm afraid so," Yuck replied. "**ATCHOO!**
I don't think I'm well enough to go to
school today."

Yuck's sister, Polly Princess, ran in. She
was dressed in her coat, woolly hat,
scarf and gloves.

"School's cancelled," Polly said, excitedly.

"Cancelled?" Yuck asked.

"Because of the snow," Polly told him.

"What snow?"

No one had told Yuck about school being cancelled or about any snow.

Yuck jumped out of bed and opened his curtains. Outside, the garden was completely white. The grass, the bushes, the trees and the treehouse were all covered in snow.

"Brilliant! Let's play snowballs!" Yuck said. "**ATCHOO!**"

"You can't play in the snow if you've got a cold," Polly told him.

"Polly's right, Yuck," Mum said. "If you're not well, you'll have to stay indoors."

Yuck wiped his runny nose on his
pyjama sleeve. "But Mum, I think my cold
has gone now. I'm feeling much better.
Please can I go outside and play?"

Mum inspected
Yuck's nose. Snot
was pouring from
it. "There'll be no
snow for you, Yuck.
Your nose is
running and you're
sneezing. You're
to stay indoors and
keep warm."

Mum stripped
the snotty green
duvet from Yuck's
bed and took it away to wash.

Polly stuck her tongue out at Yuck.
"Have a nice time indoors," she said. "I'm
off to play in the snow."

She giggled, then zipped up her coat and
headed downstairs.

Yuck looked out of his bedroom window. He saw Polly run out from the back door into the garden. She began gathering a ball of snow, rolling it across the ground. She rolled it round and round in circles, making it bigger and bigger. When it was almost too big to push, she stood it in the middle of the garden.

Yuck opened his window. "What are you doing?" he called down.

Polly looked up. "I'm making a snowman. Go away!"

"Can I help?" Yuck asked.

"No you can't!" Polly said. She smiled.
"YOU have to stay indoors!"

Polly bent down and started rolling
another ball of snow, making her
snowman's head.

Yuck changed out of his pyjamas and put on his coat, scarf and gloves. He crept out of his bedroom, then tiptoed downstairs.

Dad was in the hallway speaking on the telephone. "I'm afraid I won't be able to come into work today. My car won't start. It's covered in snow."

Yuck crept behind Dad then raced through the kitchen. He peered out of the back door and saw Polly lifting her snowman's head onto its body.

Yuck sneaked outside and hid behind a snowy bush. He watched Polly patting her

snowman, making it shiny and smooth.

Yuck picked up a handful of snow and scrunched it into a ball. It was time to play snowballs!

As Polly stood back to admire her
snowman, Yuck threw the snowball over
the garden.

It splatted Polly
on the back.

"Aaaargh!"
Polly yelled.
She looked
around. "Who
threw that?"

She looked up at Yuck's bedroom
window, brushing the snow from her coat,
but Yuck's window was closed.

Yuck giggled behind the snowy bush,
watching as Polly stomped indoors. She
came out carrying her pink dressing-up box.

Polly began dressing her snowman in a
pink scarf and a yellow flowery hat. She
put three pink buttons down its front, and
gave it two black buttons for eyes. For a
mouth she used a piece of red ribbon. Then
she pushed a carrot into her snowman's
face for a nose.

Yuck picked up another handful of snow. As he scrunched it, snot leaked from his nose and dribbled onto the snowball. The

green snot and the white snowball mixed together.

Rockits! Yuck thought. A snotball!

He threw the snotball over the garden and it landed on Polly's head.

"Aaaaargh!" Polly yelled. She span around. "Who threw that?"

Yuck was giggling. He watched as Polly took off her hat and inspected it. "Uuuuurgh!" she cried. "It's all snotty!"

Her woolly hat was sticky and green.

"**ATCHOO!**" Yuck sneezed. His sneeze shook the snow from the bush and Polly saw him.

"Yuck! It's you!" she screamed. "You're not allowed outside! You've got a cold!"

Yuck stood up. Snot was running from his nose, freezing into a long green icicle. "I was only playing," he told her. He walked over and stood beside Polly. "Can I help you with your snowman?" he asked.

"Go away, Yuck," she said. "Or I'm telling Mum."

From her dressing-up box, Polly took out a magic fairy wand and put it in her snowman's hand.

"That looks silly," Yuck said. "Snowmen don't have fairy wands."

"This is a fairy snowman," Polly told him.

"A fairy snowman?"

"Yes," Polly said. "It's magic. It can make wishes come true."

Polly turned to her fairy snowman, then closed her eyes and made a wish. "I wish Yuck would go away!"

While Polly's eyes were closed, Yuck pulled the carrot from the fairy snowman's face and swapped it with the snotty green icicle from his nose. He smiled. That looks much better, he thought.

Polly opened her eyes and saw what he'd done. "UUUURGH!" she cried. "You're DISGUSTING, Yuck!"

Polly ran indoors to get Mum.

Yuck could hear her yelling. Then he
saw the back door open and Mum came
out. Yuck quickly ducked behind Polly's
snowman.

"Yuck, where are you?" Mum called.

"He was here a minute ago," Polly said.

"**ATCHOO!**"

"What was that noise?" Mum asked.

"**ATCHOO!**"

Mum walked over and found Yuck
hiding behind Polly's fairy snowman.
"Yuck! Come out from there."

Yuck stood up, giggling.

"I told you to stay
indoors," Mum said.

"But my cold's
better now, Mum."

Yuck wiped his nose
on his sleeve, but his
nostrils were leaking
like two snotty taps.

"Don't lie, Yuck.
Come inside at once!"

Mum dragged Yuck indoors. "Go up to your bedroom and stop misbehaving!"

Yuck decided that when he was EMPEROR OF EVERYTHING, everyone would play outside in the snow, and everyone would have a runny nose – it would be the LAW. Yuck would start a massive snotball fight, firing snotballs from his freezy sneezy nose-cannon. Polly would be tied to a giant snotty icicle and get splattered in sticky green snow.

Yuck ran upstairs and closed his bedroom door. He had an idea. He sneezed into his hands. "**ATCHOO!**"

The snot was sticky and gooey. It dripped from his fingers.

"**ATCHOO! ATCHOO!**"

He sneezed again and again until his hands were full of snot.

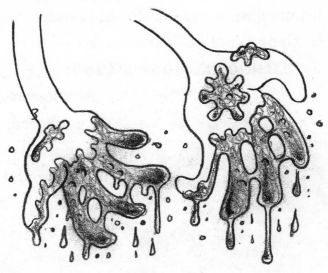

He squeezed his hands together, smoothing the snot into a sticky green ball. Then he laid the snotball on his carpet and sneezed some more.

"**ATCHOO! ATCHOO! ATCHOO!**"

A thick layer of snot covered Yuck's bedroom floor. He rolled the snotball round and round sticking more and more snot to it. It grew bigger and bigger.

"**ATCHOO! ATCHOO! ATCHOO!**"

With both hands, he pushed the sticky snotball over toenail clippings, sweet wrappers and belly-button fluff.

"**ATCHOO! ATCHOO! ATCHOO!**"

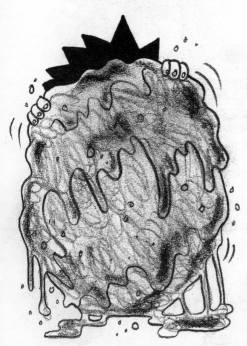

All afternoon Yuck sneezed, rolling the snotball round and round until it was as big as he was.

Yuck stood the snotball in the middle of his room then started work on another.

"ATCHOO! ATCHOO! ATCHOO!"

Again and again he sneezed, making a second snotball as big as his head.

Yuck placed the second snotball on top of the first then fetched two bouncy-ball eyeballs from under his bed. He stuck them to it. From his jokes collection he took a fake dog poo and stuck it on as a nose. Next, he peeled an old plaster from his floor and stuck it on to make a mouth.

Rockits! Yuck thought. He'd made his very own snotman!

Yuck gave the snotman three scabs for buttons, a black Superspy hat and a string of smelly socks for a scarf.

There was a knock at his door. "Yuck, Mum says it's time for dinner!" It was Polly.

"Go away. I'm busy," Yuck called.

Yuck's door burst open as Polly stomped in. She saw his snotman. "UUURGH! That's REVOLTING," she said. "I'm telling Mum."

Polly raced downstairs to the kitchen, and Yuck ran after her. "Mum, Yuck's made something disgusting in his room," Polly said.

"No, I haven't, Mum," Yuck told her.

"Sit down, both of you," Mum ordered. She placed two bowls of hot soup on the table.

Dad was already eating his. "So have you had a nice day in the snow, Polly?" he asked.

"Yes, Dad. I built a fairy snowman. It makes my wishes come true."

"And what about you, Yuck? What have you been doing today?"

"I wasn't allowed out," Yuck told him.

"Yuck's been making something disgusting in his room," Polly said.

"**ATCHOO!**" Yuck sneezed, spraying green snot into Polly's soup.

"Uurrgghh!" Polly screamed.

"Yuck, that's revolting!" Dad said.

"I can't help it. I've got a cold," Yuck said, wiping his nose on the tablecloth. "In fact, I think I'd better go back to bed."

Yuck jumped down from the table and ran out of the kitchen.

"Not so fast, Yuck," Mum called. "Tell me what you've been making upstairs."

Yuck raced back up to his room. He could hear Mum running up the stairs behind him. Quickly, he dragged his snotman into the wardrobe to hide it. He closed the wardrobe door then stood in front of it.

Mum came in and looked around. What have you been making, Yuck?" she asked.

Dad and Polly came in after her.

"Where is it?" Polly demanded.

"Where's what?" Yuck asked.

"It was here earlier. I saw it," Polly said. "It was big and green and sticky."

"Big and green and sticky?" Dad asked.

"It was a snotman!" Polly said.

"I don't know what she's talking about," Yuck said. "There's no snotman in here."

Mum looked under Yuck's bed then behind his curtains. "Hmm… I can't see anything."

"Polly, you mustn't tell fibs," Dad said. "It's not nice trying to get your brother into trouble."

Dad took hold of Polly's hand. "Come on, you. It's time for bed."

Yuck giggled as Mum and Dad led Polly away to her room.

When they'd gone, he opened his wardrobe door.

"We mustn't let them find you," he whispered to his snotman. "From now on, you're top secret."

Yuck grabbed a pair of Supercool Sunglasses from his drawer and put them on his snotman. "You're a top-secret supercool snotman," he said.

Yuck smiled then closed the wardrobe door, hiding the supercool snotman inside.

That night, Yuck dreamed that all his friends were supercool snotmen. School was cancelled forever and, instead, snotmen came to his house to play. They watched Snot TV, played snotball pool and drank snot shakes. It was a SUPERCOOL SNOTFEST!

Yuck woke up in the middle of the night. Everyone was fast asleep. He opened his curtains and looked out of the window. The moon was shining on the snow in the garden, making it glisten. Polly's fairy snowman was standing in the middle of the white lawn holding its magic wand.

"I wish I had someone fun to play with," Yuck said.

At that moment, the fairy snowman's wand began sparkling.

Yuck heard a creaking sound behind him and looked round. The door to his wardrobe was opening. A smiling snotty face peered out.

"Wow!" Yuck said.

His supercool snotman was alive!

Yuck stared in amazement as the supercool snotman stepped from the wardrobe, squelching its big snotty feet on the carpet. It smiled with its plaster mouth.

Yuck smiled back. "Hello," he said. "I'm Yuck."

The supercool snotman shook Yuck's hand. Its fingers felt sticky and gooey.

The supercool snotman stepped to Yuck's bedroom door.

"Where are you going?" Yuck whispered.

It lifted its sunglasses, then winked and tiptoed out of Yuck's room.

Yuck grabbed his coat and scarf and followed it down the stairs. The supercool snotman squelched through the kitchen and stepped out of the back door. Snowflakes were falling all around.

The supercool snotman ran into the garden, scooping up handfuls of snow. It threw them into the air.

"Do you want to play?" Yuck asked.

The supercool snotman nodded. It looked up at the sky then held out its hand. Yuck took hold of its sticky fingers and the supercool snotman started running.

It ran across the garden with Yuck by its side. Then it leapt high into the air.

Yuck leapt too.

They started floating upwards through the snowflakes.

They were flying!

"Wow!" Yuck said. "This is brilliant!"

Yuck held on tightly as they soared above the garden. Higher and higher they went, over the house and up into the sky, their arms outstretched.

They flew up into the snowclouds and out the other side. The moon was shining brightly. The supercool snotman smiled and pointed to a small green cloud.

"A snotcloud!" Yuck said.

They flew into it and Yuck felt tiny droplets of cool, sticky snot on his face.

They dived through the snotcloud and, below it, Yuck saw a huge green garden on the ground. It looked gooey and sticky. By the light of the moon he could see it glistening with thick juicy snot!

He could see other snotmen and other children with runny noses, skipping and jumping, playing together in the snot-filled garden.

"Rockits!" Yuck said as they flew down.

Yuck and the supercool snotman landed with a squelch in the sticky green snot. The children were sneezing and smiling, playing all kinds of snotty games. Yuck and the supercool snotman joined in.

They rode on a snotdog sledge with Bob the Flob.

They went snot skating with Daisy
Dewdrop on a frozen snotty pond.

They ate snot ices with Crusty Judy, and
built a snot igloo with Max Mucous.

Then Luke the Gloop threw a snotball, and EVERYONE joined in, having a great big snotball fight. Snotballs were flying everywhere.

"Rockits!" Yuck said, scooping up a handful of snot and throwing it at Sally the Sniff. It was the BEST FUN EVER.

Everyone was laughing and covered
in snot. All night they played outside, and
all night Yuck was happy.

Then, as the sun came up, the supercool snotman pointed to the sky.

Yuck looked up. It was getting light. It was time to go back. Soon Mum and Dad would be awake.

Yuck held the snotman's hand and they took off, soaring up through the snotcloud. They flew across the sky, then dived down through the snowflakes and landed back in Yuck's garden.

"That was brilliant!" Yuck said.

The supercool snotman smiled and began walking towards the back door.

Yuck saw Mum and Polly through the kitchen window, eating their breakfast.

He had an idea.

"Stop," he said to the supercool snotman.

Yuck stood his supercool snotman beside Polly's fairy snowman. "Stay still," he said.

Yuck grabbed
handfuls of snow
from the ground and
covered the supercool
snotman's green
body from head to
toe in snow. "You're

top-secret," Yuck said, smiling. "They won't
notice you in this disguise. Now wait here
until I give the signal."

Yuck whispered to the supercool snotman
and the supercool snotman nodded.

Yuck headed indoors.

"Where have you been?" Mum asked, as
he came into the kitchen.

"He's been playing outdoors!" Polly said.

"No, I haven't," Yuck
told her.

Polly jumped up from
the table and looked out of
the window. "Yes he has!
Look, Mum. He's been
building a snowman!"

Outside, Mum saw TWO snowmen standing in the middle of the garden: Polly's fairy snowman and another wearing sunglasses.

"Mine's much better than Yuck's," Polly said. "Yuck's is REVOLTING. It's got a poo on its face!"

"Yuck, I told you NOT to go outside," Mum said.

"But my cold's almost gone, Mum."

Yuck's nostrils were starting to crust over. They were blocked with crispy snot.

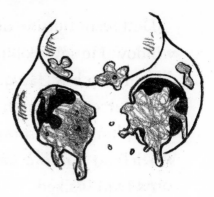

"You mustn't let him out, Mum," Polly said.

"You can't go outside until your cold has completely gone, Yuck," Mum said. "Now sit down and eat your breakfast."

Polly giggled as she picked up her dressing-up box and headed out of the back door.

"Yuck, I want you to be good today," Mum told him. "I've got better things to do than having to keep an eye on you."

Mum went out of the kitchen and Dad came in wearing a big coat. "Are you being good, Yuck?" he asked.

"Yes, Dad," Yuck replied, pouring himself a bowl of Monster Snaps.

"I'm just going to fix my car," Dad told him. "Make sure you stay indoors."

Dad went outside and Yuck ran to the window. He saw Polly rummaging in her dressing-up box. He gave the thumbs-up to his supercool snotman and it scraped a gooey handful of snow from its tummy, squelching it into a snotball.

As Dad walked round to the side gate, the supercool snotman threw the snotball, splatting Dad on the head.

Dad turned round. "Polly!" he cried. "What did you do that for?"

Polly looked up and saw Dad wiping sticky green snow from his head.

"I didn't do anything!" she said.

Yuck's supercool snotman stayed very still.

"Polly, if you can't be good you'll have to go indoors," Dad told her.

Yuck was giggling.

Just then, Mum came in carrying a broom. "Yuck, what are you doing?" she asked.

"I'm looking at the snow," Yuck told her.

"Sit down and finish your breakfast."

Yuck sat at the table, giggling.

As Mum went outside to sweep the pathway, he jumped up and ran back to the window. He saw Polly rummaging in her dressing-up box, picking out a pair of sparkly wings.

Yuck gave the thumbs up and his supercool snotman scraped a gooey handful of snow from its knee, squelching it into a snotball. The supercool snotman threw the snotball, splatting Mum on the bottom.

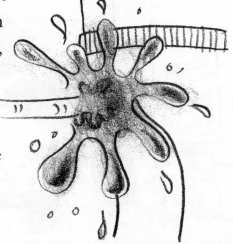

Mum turned round. "Polly!" she cried. "Why did you do that?"

Polly looked up. Mum was wiping away the sticky green snow.

"I didn't do anything!" Polly said.

Yuck's snotman stayed very still.

"Polly, if you can't be good you'll have to go indoors," Mum told her.

Yuck giggled as Mum came back inside and went to the bathroom to clean her trousers.

Yuck ran outdoors.

"Hey, you're not allowed out here, Yuck!" Polly yelled.

"I'm fine now. My cold's gone," Yuck told her.

"I'm telling on you!"

Yuck turned to his supercool snotman and gave the thumbs-up. The supercool snotman wrinkled its dog poo nose.

"ATCHOO!"

The supercool snotman sneezed, showering Polly with thick gooey snot.

"UUURGH!" she screamed.

"ATCHOO!"

The supercool snotman sneezed again, splattering Polly from head to toe. The snotman's sneezes shook off its snowy disguise. As Polly wiped her eyes she saw it standing in front of her.

"That's not a snowman!" she cried. "That's a snotman! And it's alive!"

Yuck was laughing. Polly was dripping with snot.

"I hate you, Yuck!" she screamed.

Yuck and the supercool snotman raced across the garden.

Polly chased after them.

"Quick, hide!" Yuck said.

They climbed the rope ladder to the treehouse.

"Yuck, come down from there!" Polly screamed. "You're in BIG TROUBLE."

Yuck peered through the slats in the treehouse floor. Polly was standing below, all gooey and green.

"I'm telling on you!" she spluttered.

Yuck looked up. Between the wooden planks on the roof of the treehouse he could see a thick layer of snow. He turned to the supercool snotman then tapped his nose. "Ready… Steady…"

"AAAAAAAAAATCHHHOOOOOOOOOOOOOO!"

Two huge jets of snot blasted the walls of
the treehouse as Yuck and the supercool
snotman both let out an almighty sneeze.
The treehouse shook and the snow began
sliding from the roof.

"Aaaggghhh!" Polly screamed.

Yuck looked down as a huge mound of
snow landed on
top of Polly.

"That'll teach
her!" Yuck said
to his supercool
snotman.

Yuck smiled then climbed down. He stood by the mound of snow. He could hear Polly shouting inside it. "It's f-f-freezing in here! I h-h-hate you, Yuck!"

He raced across the garden. "Mum, Dad," he called.

Mum came running out from the back door. Dad came running round from the side gate.

"What on earth was that noise?" Dad asked.

"It sounded like a big sneeze," Mum said. "Yuck, what are you doing outside?"

"It wasn't me who sneezed, Mum," he told her. "My cold's gone."

 Mum checked Yuck's nostrils. All Yuck's snot had vanished. His big sneeze had blown it away.

"Then who did sneeze?" she asked.

"There was a snotman out here," Yuck told her. "It's okay, though. I've captured it."

"A snotman?" Dad asked. "Yuck, what on earth are you talking about?"

Yuck pointed across the garden. There were sticky green footprints leading to a large mound of snow beneath the treehouse. The mound of snow was shaking and shivering.

"Be careful," Yuck said. "The snotman's under there. It could attack at any moment!"

"Stand back," Dad said. "I'll deal with this."

As Dad approached the mound of snow, it began trembling.

Suddenly, it exploded with sneezes. "**ATCHOO! ATCHOO! ATCHOO!**"

"URRRGHH!" Mum and Dad screamed, as they got splattered.

Standing in front of them was a green creature. It was angry-looking and dripping with snot.

"Wait a minute," Dad said, wiping his face. "That's not a snotman!"

The creature was shivering.

"That's Polly!" Mum said.

Polly sneezed. "**ATCHOO! ATCHOO!**"

"Oh dear," Yuck said. "It looks like she's caught a cold."

Polly sneezed again. "**ATCHOO!**"

"Perhaps you'd better take her indoors."

"Polly, come inside!" Mum told her.

"But, Mum—"

Yuck was giggling. "Polly, you can't play in the snow if you've got a cold."

"I HATE you, Yuck!" Polly said. "**ATCHOO!**"
As Mum and Dad led Polly back to the
house, Yuck gave the thumbs up to his
supercool snotman and it climbed down
from the treehouse.

Yuck scooped up
a handful of snow.
"Let's play snowballs!"

YUCK'S DREAM MACHINE

Yuck had seen the Dream Machine featured in his comic *OINK*. It was the **Five-Star Brilliant Buy of the Month**. He'd saved up ALL his pocket money and sent off for it. Now it was finally his!

Yuck opened the box excitedly, and took out a cone-shaped object dotted with coloured lights. It had a transmitter aerial on its top and a small door on its side with the words: **ADD YOUR INGREDIENTS HERE...**

Yuck read the instructions:

**Make your own dreams with
the DREAM MACHINE. Simply
add your favourite ingredients,
turn it on and close your eyes!**

Yuck couldn't wait to try it. He fetched a
plastic beetle, a rubber millipede and two
glow-in-the-dark flies from his bug
collection. He opened the door on the
dream machine and popped them inside.

He switched the dream machine on and the lights started flashing. The transmitter at the top began whirling round and round. Yuck placed the dream machine by the side of his bed, then lay down and closed his eyes. Soon he was asleep.

The dream machine sent a signal to Yuck's brain. He started dreaming he was a bug-sized explorer...

He was tiny, as small as an insect, and he set off on a brilliant bug adventure.

Yuck dreamed that he was running through the grass, racing a millipede. It had hundreds of feet and was the fastest runner ever! But when it stopped to tie its laces, Yuck overtook, zooming past.

He skidded through slug-slime and mingled with maggots, then climbed up

onto a spider's web. He bounced up and down. It was like jumping on a trampoline! He shot upwards and landed on a fly, soaring high into the air.

The fly was sniffing. It could smell something stinky. It flew down and landed on a poo, then began licking it and rubbing its legs together.

Yuck slid down the side of the poo and played stink-chase with a dung beetle, running round and round and round.

In the morning, Mum came into Yuck's room. "Yuck," she said. "It's time to get up." She looked at Yuck. He was asleep in bed. He was wriggling like a worm.

Yuck was still dreaming. In his dream, he was deep underground exploring worm tunnels and getting covered in mud. Yuck licked his fingers. Wow! The mud tasted like chocolate!

Just then, Yuck dreamed something was
tugging at him. He looked round and saw
a claw dragging him from the worm tunnel.

"Wake up!" he heard.

Yuck saw a monster reaching for him.
It looked like Mum, except it was big and
hairy. It had sharp claws and pointy fangs.

"Wake up, Yuck!" it roared.

Yuck dreamed that he threw a lasso over the monster. Then he dreamed up a big cage and dragged the monster inside.

Yuck half-opened his eyes.

Mum was shouting in his ear. "Wake up, Yuck!"

"M-m-m-monster!" Yuck said when he saw her.

"What are you talking about, Yuck?" Mum asked.

Yuck rubbed his eyes and looked around. "I… I… I was dreaming," he said.

Mum had woken him up. "Get up, Yuck, or you'll be late for school."

"But, Mum. Can't I sleep a bit longer?"

"Yuck, I want you downstairs and ready in five minutes," Mum told him.

As Mum left the room, Yuck glanced at the dream machine beside his bed. Dreams are much more fun than school, he thought. Perhaps he'd have just one more dream before he got up.

Yuck reached under his bed, looking for more ingredients. He found a pot of slime and a pair of dirty underpants. He stuffed them into the dream machine, then switched it on. The lights started flashing. Yuck snuggled down and closed his eyes.

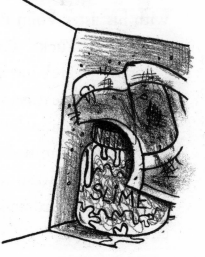

He dreamed that he was a superslimy
superhero wearing a pair of dirty
underpants. He flew through the air over
Slime City, splatting
baddies with his
superslimy powers.

While Yuck was still asleep, Mum and
Dad were downstairs eating their breakfast
with his sister, Polly Princess.

"Where's Yuck?" Polly asked.

"He's just getting up," Mum said.
"He'd better not make me late
for school," Polly moaned. "Miss
Fortune is reading us a story today
and I want to sit at the front."

Dad got up from his chair. "I'll go and
check," he said.

But when Dad went upstairs to Yuck's room, he found Yuck asleep in bed. Yuck's arms were stretched out in front of him as if he was flying. "Wake up, Yuck," Dad said.

Yuck dreamed that a monster was reaching for him. It looked like Dad except it had tentacles instead of arms. Its mouth opened and Yuck saw row upon row of razor-sharp teeth. The monster snapped its jaws: "Wake up!"

Yuck dreamed that he dived down and blasted the monster with his super-gloopy

slime-ray. The monster slipped and slid as Yuck dragged it into the big metal cage where the Mum monster was held. He locked the cage shut.

Yuck half-opened his eyes. Dad was shouting in his ear. "Wake up, Yuck!"

"M-m-m-monster!" Yuck said when he saw Dad.

"What are you talking about, Yuck?" Dad asked.

Yuck rubbed his eyes and looked around. "I... I... I was dreaming," he said.

"You're to get up NOW, Yuck," Dad told him, opening the curtains. "You can't lie in bed all day."

"But Dad, I like it in bed. Can't I sleep a bit longer?"

"I want you downstairs and ready to leave in thirty seconds!" Dad said.

As Dad left the room, Yuck glanced at the dream machine, thinking of all the fantastic dreams he could have. He wanted to go on adventures in Spiderland and Toenail Town. He was just reaching under his bed for some old toenail clippings when Polly Princess came storming in.

"Yuck, hurry up and get out of bed. I don't want to be late for school."

"Go away, Polly," Yuck said. "I'm busy."

Polly snatched the dream machine from beside his bed. "What's this?" she asked.

"Give that back," Yuck said.

Polly was twiddling the transmitter on its top. "Tell me what it is or I'll break it."

"It's my dream machine," Yuck said. "I got it from *OINK*."

"A dream machine! I want a go!"

"Hands off," Yuck told her, taking it back.

Polly stuck her tongue out, then ran from Yuck's room. "Mum, Dad, he's still in bed!"

"Yuck, GET UP NOW!" Mum and Dad yelled from the kitchen.

Yuck quickly got up and pulled on his clothes. He put the dream machine in his school bag, then rushed downstairs and opened the front door. "Get a move on, Polly," he said. "I've been ready for ages."

Mum and Dad looked at Polly sternly. "Hurry up, Polly, your brother's waiting for you."

Yuck giggled then left with Polly for school.

When Yuck arrived in class, Mrs Wagon the Dragon was standing at the front. "Today we're going do long division," she announced.

Yuck crept along the line of desks.

"You're late, Yuck!" the Dragon boomed.

She stormed over and whacked him with her umbrella.

"Sorry, Miss. It wasn't my fault," he said. "My mum and dad forgot to wake me up."

"Don't be ridiculous!" the Dragon said, and she booted Yuck to the back of the class.

BOOT

Yuck landed in his seat beside Little Eric. He took the dream machine from his bag. "Look what I've got," he whispered.

"Cool!" Little Eric said. "A dream machine! Let's have a go!"

"You just need to add an ingredient," Yuck told him.

Little Eric opened the door of the dream machine and saw the underpants, the bugs and the slime inside. He thought for a moment then rummaged in his bag. "Will this work?" he asked, passing Yuck a stinkbomb.

"Brilliant!" Yuck said. "A stinky dream!"

Yuck popped the stinkbomb into the dream machine, then switched it on. The lights started flashing and the transmitter whirled round and round.

Yuck and Little Eric lay back in their seats and closed their eyes. In no time at all they were asleep at the back of the class.

While the Dragon was droning on with her lesson, Yuck and Little Eric began dreaming…

They dreamed they were in a fart factory. Big bottom-shaped machines were rumbling all around them. They loaded the machines with beans, cabbage, onions and cheese. The machines rumbled louder, parping and trumpeting, letting off gas.

Yuck was the Chief Maker of Farts, pulling levers, turning dials and pressing buttons, creating the smelliest farts in the universe.

Little Eric was the Head of Quality Control, sniffing the farts to make sure they were stinky enough. They made HONKERS and SQUIDGERS, BLASTERS and SNEEKERS. The farts shot along tubes and whizzed out from curly pipes gathering in a big smelly cloud.

While Yuck and Little Eric were dreaming, Mrs Wagon the Dragon was marching up and down at the front of the class, calling out sums. "What is one hundred and twelve divided by eight?"

Everyone in the class was sniffing.

"Come on! What's the answer?"

"Phwoargh!" Schoolie Julie said.

"What's that stink?" Tall Paul asked.

Everyone turned in their seats and saw Yuck and Little Eric at the back of the class. They were snoring and farting!

Zzz… zzz… **PARP!**… zzz…**TRUMP!**

"Wake up, NOW!" the Dragon shouted, running over to them. "Stop that at once!"

But Yuck and Little Eric were fast asleep. They dreamed that a monster stormed into the fart factory. It looked like Mrs Wagon but had dragon wings and was breathing fire. "Wake up!" it roared.

Yuck pulled a tube from a fart machine and pointed it at the monster.

Little Eric aimed another.

PAAAAARP!
TRUUUMP!

Two huge stinky farts shot from the ends of the tubes straight into the monster's face. Its eyes swirled then it wobbled and fell to the ground.

Quickly, Yuck and Little Eric dragged the monster from the fart factory and stuffed it into the cage where the Mum monster and the Dad monster were held.

Yuck and Little Eric half-opened their eyes. The Dragon was leaning over their desks, coughing. "Wake up!"

"M-m-m-monster!" Yuck said when he saw her.

The Dragon's eyes were watering. "What do you think you're doing?" she demanded.

Yuck sniffed. The classroom stank of farts! He rubbed his eyes and looked around. All the children were pinching their noses.

"I… I… I was dreaming Miss," Yuck said.

Little Eric rubbed his eyes. "It was fart-tastic, Miss," he said.

"I'll have none of that in my class!" the Dragon boomed. "You're to see the headmaster at once!"

Yuck quickly took the dream machine from his desk and hid it in his bag. The Dragon whacked Yuck and Little Eric with her umbrella, then dragged them up the corridor to Mr Reaper the headmaster's office.

She knocked on the Reaper's door. "Mr Reaper, these boys were sleeping in my lesson," she said. "And they were farting too!"

"Sit them on The Bench," the Reaper replied. "I'll deal with them in a moment."

The Dragon sat Yuck and Little Eric on The Bench outside the Reaper's office then stormed off back to her class.

Yuck and Little Eric hated The Bench. The Bench was where people sat before they got into BIG TROUBLE.

"What are we going to do?" Little Eric asked.

Yuck took the dream machine from his bag. "How about we have a little sleep?"

Yuck looked for something yucky to dream about. In the bin outside the headmaster's office he found half a mouldy sandwich and a crisp packet. He popped them inside the dream machine, then switched it on.

Yuck and Little Eric closed their eyes.

They dreamed that they were stuffing their faces with food, taking a ride on the VOMITRON. It was the world's fastest, most stomach-churning rollercoaster.

Yuck and Little Eric were scoffing sandwiches and crunching crisps, hurtling up and down a looping track. They were laughing and shaking, their stomachs heaving with every bend.

While Yuck and Little Eric were
dreaming, the Reaper came out of his
office. He saw them asleep on The Bench,
rolling from side to side with their eyes
closed and with smiles on their faces.

"Wake up!" the Reaper said.

But Yuck and Little Eric were having too
much fun to wake up. They dreamed that
the VOMITRON was racing at one
hundred miles an hour, twisting and
turning, mixing the food in their stomachs.

As the VOMITRON did a loop-the-loop… UUURRRGGGHHH!… Yuck and Little Eric were sick!

"Wake up!" they heard.

Yuck and Little Eric licked their lips. They dreamed that a monster was sitting between them on the rollercoaster. It looked like the Reaper except it was nobbly with long horns. It was covered in sick and looked angry.

It roared: "Wake up!"

Yuck quickly pulled the brake lever on the rollercoaster and the monster shot out of its seat. Little Eric dived onto it and they dragged it into the cage with the other monsters, locking it up.

Yuck and Little Eric half-opened their eyes. Standing in front of them was the Reaper. He had sick on his trousers and shoes.

"Wake up!" he shouted.

"M-m-m-monster!" Yuck and Little Eric said when they saw him.

"What do you think you're doing?" the Reaper demanded.

Yuck rubbed his eyes and sat up. "I... I... I... was dreaming," he said.

Little Eric rubbed his eyes. "It was amazing, Sir," he said.

The Reaper wiped his shoes with a tissue. "You two are in BIG TROUBLE!"

He dragged Yuck and Little Eric down the corridor, and fetched a broom and a rubbish bag from Mr Sweep the caretaker's cupboard. "As punishment, I'm putting you both on litter duty this lunchtime!"

"But, Sir—"

"No buts! If you're going to make a mess, then you can do some cleaning up!"

That lunchtime, Yuck and Little Eric had to go round the school sweeping up and collecting litter.

Polly Princess and Juicy Lucy saw them in the playground and came running over.

"In trouble, are you?" Polly said, giggling.

"No," Yuck told her.

"Then how come you're on litter duty?"

She pointed to the broom and the rubbish bag.

"Oh, these," Yuck said. "The Reaper asked us to give these to you. We're just off for a snooze."

Yuck and Little Eric handed the broom and the bag to Polly and Lucy, then walked off laughing.

"I'm telling!" Polly called.

Yuck and Little Eric ran to the edge of the playground. Fartin Martin and Tom Bum were standing by the bushes, picking their noses.

Yuck took out the dream machine from his bag.

"Awesome!" Fartin Martin said, looking at it. "Can I have a go?"

"Me too," Tom Bum said.

Yuck, Fartin Martin, Tom Bum and Little Eric hid behind the bushes.

"We'll need something to dream about," Yuck told them.

Everyone looked in their pockets. Yuck
found a packet of Blowers
Bubblegum and put a piece in
the machine. Fartin
Martin put in a
World Wrestling
Mania collector's
card. Tom Bum put in a
squashed piece of chocolate
cake. Little Eric
 added a Mega Magic
stick-on tattoo and a
small scab from his knee.

Yuck switched on the dream machine
and placed it on the ground. They lay
down and closed their eyes. Soon they were
all dreaming…

Yuck dreamed they went bubblegum burp bowling. They all blew big bubblegum bowling balls and rolled them down a bowling alley, knocking over skittles. **BURP** went the bubbles as they burst.

Fartin Martin dreamed they landed in a wrestling ring. A crowd was cheering. It was World Wrestling Mania! They wrestled with The Karate King, Mr Mega, Hero Hercules and The Boneshaker. And they all won! They were World Wrestling champions!

Tom Bum dreamed they went to the world's best restaurant to celebrate. Instead of eating the food, they decided to throw it at each other. They threw chocolate cake, treacle tart and spaghetti, and had the biggest food fight ever! They were all covered from head to toe in food.

Then Little Eric dreamed that a huge scab flew in the window. They hopped onto it like a flying carpet and soared over a magical city. They all had Mega Magic powers! Yuck zapped Fartin Martin and turned him into a frog. Fartin Martin croaked and turned Tom Bum into a hippopotamus. Tom Bum belched and turned Little Eric into a mouse. Little Eric squeaked and turned Yuck into a gorilla. Yuck beat his chest and grunted, and they all turned back into themselves again.

It was the BEST DREAM EVER! All afternoon, they lay behind the bushes, sleeping and dreaming and laughing. They were having so much fun that by the time they woke up, hours had passed.

"That was awesome!" Fartin Martin said, rubbing his eyes.

"I'm going to get one of those machines!" Tom Bum said.

"Me too!" Little Eric said.

They crept out from behind the bushes. All the children were heading home.

School was over!

Polly stood at the school gates, waiting for Yuck. "Yuck, where have you been?" she asked. "Everyone's been looking for you."

"I've been busy," Yuck said.

Polly saw him putting the dream machine into his bag. "No, you haven't! You've been sleeping!" she said. "Just you wait! I'm telling Mum."

That evening at home, Yuck raced straight upstairs to his room.

There was a knock on his door. Mum came in with Polly behind her.

"What's this about you sleeping at school?" Mum asked.

"I don't know what you're talking about," Yuck said.

"Yes, you do," Polly told him. "You've been snoozing all day."

"Have you, Yuck?" Mum asked.

Polly grabbed Yuck's school bag and took out his dream machine. "This is why, Mum."

"Give that back," Yuck said.

Polly handed the dream machine to Mum.

"What on earth is this thing?" Mum asked, looking at it.

"It's a dream machine," Polly said. "He got it from *OINK*."

Mum looked at Yuck. "I'm confiscating this," she told him. "You're not allowed to play with it anymore."

"But Mum—"

"I'll not have you sleeping all day. It's LAZY! You can stay in your room and get on with your homework for a change."

Mum walked out, taking Yuck's dream machine with her.

"It serves you right for not giving me a go," Polly said. She giggled, then followed Mum downstairs.

Yuck decided that when he was EMPEROR OF EVERYTHING, everyone would sleep all day long. It would be the LAW. At school, everyone would snooze in class and prizes would be awarded for whoever had the best dream. Polly would be sent to the back of the class because she'd only ever have NIGHTMARES!

All evening, Yuck had to stay in his room pretending to do his homework. He tried snoozing, but it wasn't much fun without his dream machine. All he could think of was how to get it back.

When it was bedtime, he crept downstairs and tiptoed to the kitchen. He looked in the cupboard where Mum usually hid the things she confiscated. His dream machine wasn't there.

Yuck looked in the living room and in the hallway, and even in the bathroom. But his dream machine was nowhere to be seen. Then he saw Polly coming out of her bedroom.

"What are you doing?" Polly demanded. "You're meant to be in your room."

"Where's my dream machine?" Yuck asked.

"I've no idea. Perhaps Mum threw it in the dustbin."

Polly grinned, then pushed past Yuck, heading to the bathroom to clean her teeth.

Polly's bedroom
door was open.

Yuck peered inside.

His dream
machine was on
her bedside table!
Polly had stolen it!

Quickly, Yuck popped a pink ribbon
inside it and switched it on. He lay down
and closed his eyes. In no time at all he
was dreaming...

Yuck dreamed of the cage full of monsters.

He dreamed that the cage began turning into an enormous pink present. He wrapped it in pink wrapping paper and tied a pink ribbon around it, then he attached a note.

This was going to be fun!

Yuck woke up smiling. He could hear Polly gargling in the bathroom. Quickly, he put the dream machine back beside her bed.

Polly came in. "What are you doing in my room?" she asked.

"I was just looking for my dream machine," Yuck told her. "But I couldn't find it anywhere."

"Go away!" Polly said. "I'm going to sleep."

Yuck walked out smiling, and Polly closed the door behind him.

When Yuck had left, Polly rushed to her bed. The dream machine was finally HERS!

She opened the door on its front and filled the machine with pink petals, a pink fairy wand and sparkling pink glitter.

She switched on the dream machine, then lay down and closed her eyes.

Polly dreamed she was in a world full of pink flowers. Pink fairies were flying from petal to petal, their pink wings sparkling. Polly dreamed that she had wings too. She flew up into a pink sky with fluffy pink clouds and a pretty pink sun.

Polly flew for miles and miles over a
magical pink land, where everything was
pretty and nice. It was the most beautiful
dream she'd ever had.

Then she saw an enormous pink present
on the ground. It was as big as a house.

She flew down to it.

The present
was wrapped in
pink paper and
tied with a pink
ribbon. On it
was a note:

to Polly
Sweet Dreams
from Yuck

Polly undid
the ribbon
and tore off
the wrapping
paper…

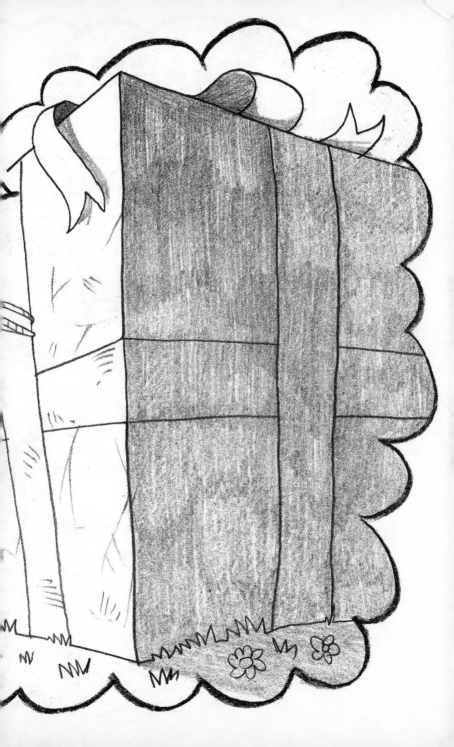

A stream of monsters burst out!

A monster with sharp claws pinched her.
Another monster wrapped its tentacles
around her. A monster with horns charged
at her. It was covered in sick. A dragon
monster roared at her, breathing fire.

"HELP!" Polly screamed. "MONSTERS!"

Mum and Dad came running to Polly's room.

"Polly, what on earth's the matter?" Mum cried.

Yuck peered in through Polly's door. She was sitting up in bed, shaking.

"What happened?" Dad asked her.

Polly's face was white with shock. She could hardly speak. "M– M– M– MONSTERS!" she said.

Mum saw the Dream Machine flashing beside her bed. "Polly, what are you doing with that?"

Yuck was laughing. "Oh dear, Polly," he said. "Did you have a bad dream?"

Become a member of Yuck's fanclub at:

WWW.YUCKWEB.COM

Find Matt and Dave's rotten jokes, gross games and disgusting downloads, as well as crazy competitions AND the first word on Yuck's new adventures.

Be warned: it's really Yucky!